JAPAN

Tracy Vonder Brink

TABLE OF CONTENTS

Japan 3
Glossary 22
Index 24

A Crabtree Seedlings Book

School-to-Home Support for Caregivers and Teachers

This book helps children grow by letting them practice reading. Here are a few guiding questions to help the reader with building his or her comprehension skills. Possible answers appear here in red.

Before Reading:

- What do I think this book is about?
    - *I think this book is about Japan.*
    - *I think this book is about ways of life in Japan.*

- What do I want to learn about this topic?
    - *I want to learn about the weather in Japan.*
    - *I want to learn about traditional clothing in Japan.*

During Reading:

- I wonder why...
    - *I wonder why Japan has an emperor.*
    - *I wonder why there are so many temples in Japan.*

- What have I learned so far?
    - *I have learned that Japan is made up of many islands.*
    - *I have learned that Kyoto is one of Japan's oldest cities.*

After Reading:

- What details did I learn about this topic?
    - *I have learned that Tokyo is the capital of Japan.*
    - *I have learned that the Tokyo Skytree is one of the tallest buildings in the world.*

- Read the book again and look for the vocabulary words.
    - *I see the word **emperor** on page 8, and the word **bamboo** on page 18. The other glossary words are on pages 22 and 23.*

Japan is a country.

It is in **Asia**.

Japan is made up of islands.

Tokyo is the **capital**.

It is a big city.

The Tokyo Skytree
is one of the tallest
buildings in the world.

Most people in Japan speak Japanese.

Ameyoko Market in Tokyo has hundreds of shops.

Some sell tasty snacks and meals. Others sell clothes, shoes, and other goods.

自転車専用
アメ横
庶民のアメ横 楽しい買物
アメ横商店街連合会
免税店
TAX FREE
Tax-free
マルセル
摩利支天 徳大寺
H・S・K

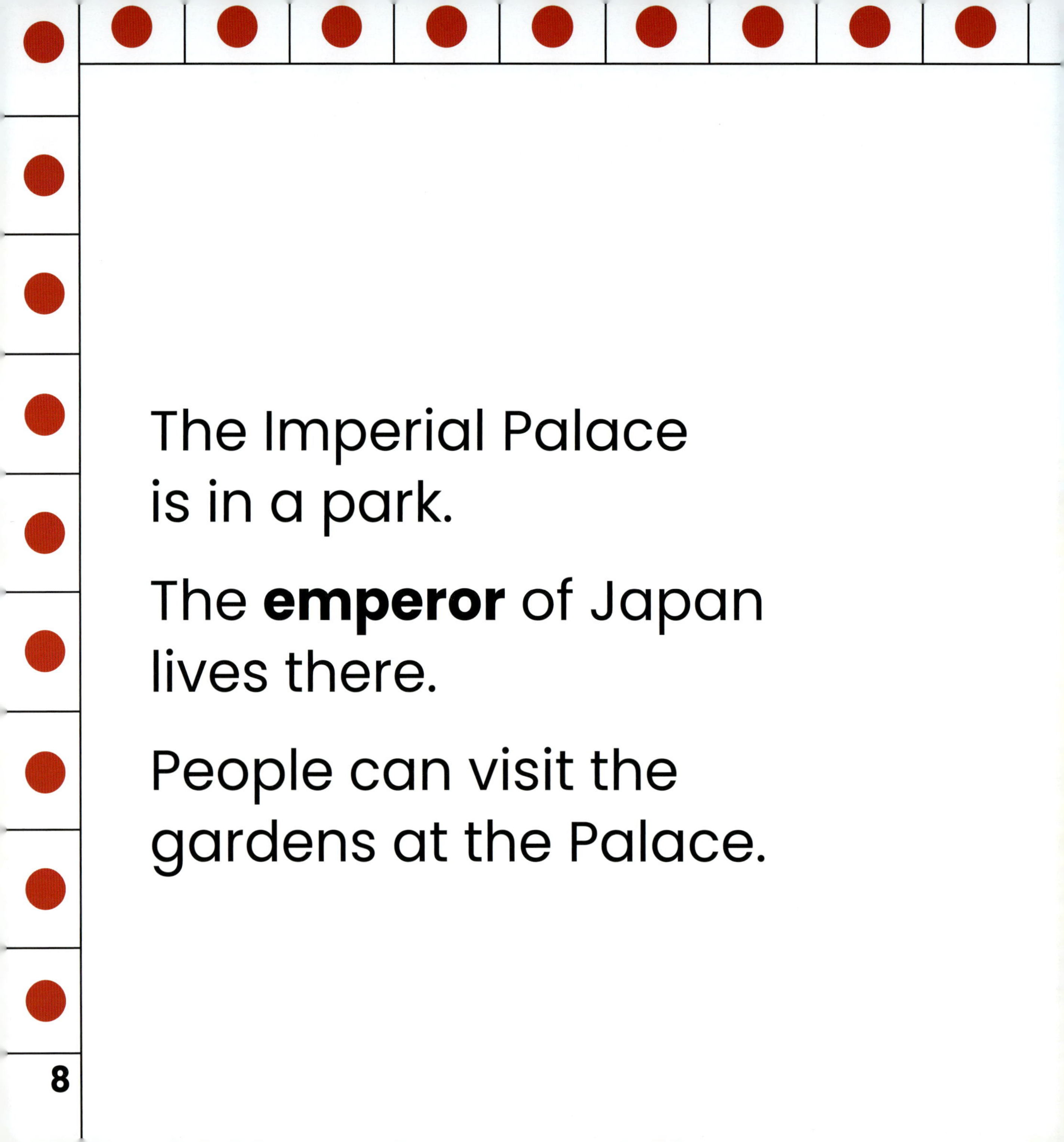

The Imperial Palace
is in a park.

The **emperor** of Japan
lives there.

People can visit the
gardens at the Palace.

Emperor Go-Komatsu was the 100th emperor of Japan, from 1392 to 1412.

Mount Fuji is the highest mountain in Japan.

It is a volcano.

Around 300,000 people climb Mount Fuji every year.

Kyoto is one of Japan's oldest cities.

It has beautiful gardens and **temples**.

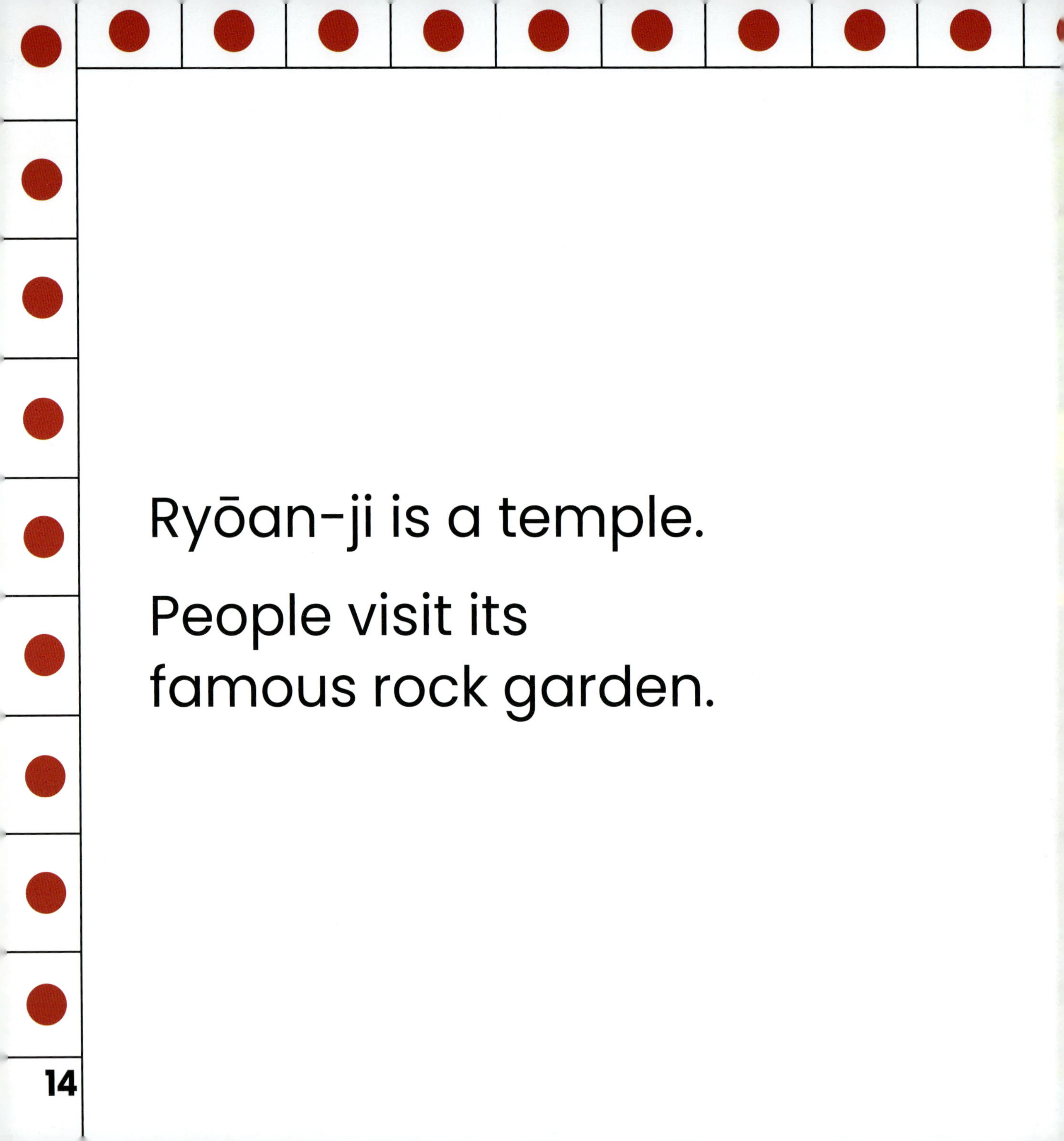

Ryōan-ji is a temple.

People visit its
famous rock garden.

Kinkaku-ji is
another temple.

Its top floors
sparkle with gold.

Kinkaku-ji means
The Golden Pavilion.

People walk through the Sagano **Bamboo** Forest.

The tall plants stretch toward the sky.

Visitors to Japan may
enjoy a tea **ceremony**.

They sit on the floor.

They drink green tea.

Japan has a lot to see and do!

Glossary

Asia (AY-zhuh): The continent between Europe and Africa on one side and the Pacific Ocean on the other

bamboo (bam-BOO): A tall plant with hard, hollow stems

capital (KAP-i-tl): The city where the government of a country or a state is located